Gertrude Chandler Warner's

THE BOXCAR CHILDREN

GRAPHIC NOVELS

THE BOXCAR CHILDREN

Henry, Jessie, Violet, and Benny are a family. They're brothers and sisters—and they're orphans, too. The only way they can stay together is to try and make it on their own. But where will they live?

One night, during a storm, the children find an old red boxcar that keeps them warm and safe. The children decide to make it their home—and they become the Boxcar Children!

THE BOXCAR CHILDREN
GRAPHIC NOVELS

Gertrude Chandler Warner's

THE BOXCAR CHILDREN

Adapted by Shannon Eric Denton
Illustrated by Mike Dubisch

Henry Alden

Watch

Jessie Alden

Violet Alden

Benny Alden

Visit us at www.albertwhitman.com.

Copyright © 2009 by Abdo Consulting Group, Inc. All rights reserved. Published in 2009 by Albert Whitman & Company, 6340 Oakton Street, Morton Grove, Illinois, 60053-2723 by arrangement with Abdo Consulting Group, Inc. No part of this book may be reproduced in any form without written permission from the publisher. THE BOXCAR CHILDREN® is a registered trademark of Albert Whitman & Company.

Adapted by Shannon Eric Denton
Illustrated by Mike Dubisch
Colored by Wes Hartman
Lettered by Kristen Fitzner Denton
Edited by Stephanie Hedlund
Interior layout and design by Kristen Fitzner Denton
Cover art by Mike Dubisch
Book design and packaging by Shannon Eric Denton

Library of Congress Cataloging-in-Publication Data

Denton, Shannon Eric.
 Boxcar children / adapted by Shannon Eric Denton; illustrated by Mike Dubisch.
    p. cm. -- (Gertrude Chandler Warner's boxcar children)
  ISBN 978-1-60270-586-9
  [1. Orphans--Fiction. 2. Family--Fiction. 3. Mystery and detective stories.] I. Dubisch, Michael, ill. II. Warner, Gertrude Chandler, 1890-1979. Boxcar children. III. Title.
  PZ7.D4373Box 2009
  [E]--dc22

                                2008036095

10 9 8 7 6 5 4 3 2

Gertrude Chandler Warner's

THE BOXCAR CHILDREN

GRAPHIC NOVELS

Contents

The Aldens walked down the road as fast as they could.

They walked and walked for a long time. Then the sun began to come up.

Look over there!

That looks good, Violet. What a big haystack!

The children were so tired they went right to sleep. They slept all day, and it was night again when they woke up.

Oh Jessie, I'm hungry. I want something to eat.

Good old Benny. We'll have supper.

Jessie took out a loaf of bread and cut it into four pieces. It was soon gone.

The children heard a horse and cart coming up the road. They hid behind some bushes.

I wonder where those children went. I don't think they could walk as far as Silver City.

Let's look a little while longer.

They were just in time. The children could hear the rain on the top of the boxcar, but no rain came in.

What a beautiful place!

Henry! Let's live here! This boxcar is a fine little house.

We'll stay here today, anyway.

I want some milk.

I'll go to the next town and get some.

Before Henry came back, Jessie heard a noise. Something was in the woods!

When Henry comes, the blueberries will be good with milk.

Where did you get that fine dog?

He came to us. He is a surprise for you. We've named him Watch.

Jessie cut the loaf of bread Henry brought into five big pieces. The cheese was cut into four pieces. Jessie gave Watch a piece of bread.

After supper, Henry made four pine needle beds in one end of the car.

This side will be the bedroom.

The kitchen will be on the other side.

Back at the brook, the girls washed the dishes with soap. Jessie used sand to get the rust off the spoons.

They used a board from the dump to make a fine shelf for the dishes.

There!

Henry returned with many funny looking bundles in his arms, but he would not open them or tell what he had been doing until it was time for dinner.

It was dinnertime and the children sat down to see what Henry had in his bundles.

Where did you get the dishes?

We went exploring and found a big dump.

I bought another loaf of brown bread and some more milk. Then I bought some dried meat, because we can eat it with our hands. And I bought a bone for Watch.

Now tell us what you did in town, Henry.

I met a man and asked him if I could cut the grass and he said yes. He was a doctor, and he gave me a dollar and this bag.

Let's have cookies for dinner.

That night the children were all asleep but Henry. He saw that Watch was not asleep. Watch growled. Then Jessie woke up. But nothing came.

At last Watch lay back down.

Maybe it was just a rabbit.

Don't tell Violet and Benny.

A BIG MEAL FROM LITTLE ONIONS

You're a good worker. Here's a dollar.

The next morning, Henry ran to the doctor's house. There, he thinned out the carrots in the doctor's garden. Mrs. Moore, the doctor's mother, watched.

Henry got to keep all the little carrots, turnips, and onions he pulled up. Then he bought some meat with the dollar Mrs. Moore gave him.

While Henry was gone, Benny and the girls made a rock fireplace. They were delighted with the meat and the little vegetables Henry brought back at lunchtime.

We can make a stew for supper tonight!

Henry wished he could stay and smell the stew boiling, but he went back to work at Dr. Moore's house.

Henry cleaned the doctor's garage that afternoon. The doctor gave him a spare hammer. He also let Henry keep all of the old nails.

I need helpers to pick the cherry trees. Come back Monday.

Henry started for home. He had another dollar, a pocket full of old nails, and a hammer.

Maybe we could all pick cherries.

For dinner, Jessie ladled out the stew into plates and bowls. The meat was well cooked, and the vegetables were delicious.

It had been a busy day, and everyone was tired. Henry went to sleep with his new hammer under his pillow.

FUN IN THE CHERRY ORCHARD

Now the pool is deep enough for all of us to swim in.

The next day was Sunday, and Henry got to stay home. The children built a dam for a swimming pool. Benny carried stones in the cart Henry had built for him.

On Monday, Henry told Jessie and Violet that Dr. Moore needed cherry pickers.

We should all go.

But we must be careful. What if our grandfather is looking for us?

They all went to Dr. Moore's. Benny carried baskets to the pickers and ate all the cherries he wanted.

Mrs. Moore loved Benny.

The children didn't know what to say when Dr. Moore invited them to stay for dinner.

Will your parents be watching for you?

No. Our mother and father are dead.

At the end of the day, the doctor gave them four dollars and all the cherries they could carry.

You have worked hard enough. Come again.

Oh my! James Henry Alden!

LOST. Four children, two boys and two girls. Somewhere around Greenfield or Silver City. Five thousand dollars to anyone who can find them. - James Henry Alden

The four children are living in a boxcar. But I won't tell Mr. Alden that they are his grandchildren.

Back at the boxcar, Jessie and Violet taught Benny to read. Henry went to work for the doctor every day.

One day, Violet became really sick.

I wish Henry would come home!

When Henry came at last, they tried to get Violet warm. But they couldn't.

I'm going to get Dr. Moore.

The doctor did not ask Henry which way to go, but the car went up the right road.

Stay here.

The doctor ran alone up the hill to the boxcar. It seemed like magic that he knew where to go.

Are you going to take her to a hospital?

No, I'm taking her to my house.

Violet was so sick that the doctor did not go to bed all night. He sat by her side until morning.

The children all slept in real beds at the doctor's house. Henry and Benny shared a big bed, Jessie slept in a little one. Benny was the first one up.

Follow me!

Mr. Alden took them by the garage and through the big gardens.

At last they came to a garden with a fountain in the middle and trees around it.

Near the fountain was the surprise.

ABOUT THE CREATOR

Gertrude Chandler Warner was born on April 16, 1890, in Putnam, Connecticut. In 1918, Warner began teaching at Israel Putnam School. As a teacher, she discovered that many readers who liked an exciting story could not find books that were both easy and fun to read. She decided to try to meet this need. In 1942, *The Boxcar Children* was published for these readers.

Warner drew on her own experience to write *The Boxcar Children*. As a child she spent hours watching trains go by on the tracks near her family home. She often dreamed about what it would be like to live in a caboose or freight car—just as the Alden children do.

When readers asked for more Alden adventures, Warner began additional stories. While the mystery element is central to each of the books, she never thought of them as strictly juvenile mysteries. She liked to stress the Aldens' independence. Henry, Jessie, Violet, and Benny go about most of their adventures with as little adult supervision as possible—something that delights young readers.

During her lifetime, Warner received hundreds of letters from fans as she continued the Aldens' adventures, writing nineteen Boxcar Children books in all. After her death in 1979, her publisher, Albert Whitman and Company, carried on Warner's vision. Today, the Boxcar Children series has more than 100 books.